PEDRO

PEDRO AND THE
SHARK

by Fran Manushkin

illustrated by
Tammie Lyon

raintree 🐾

a Capstone company — publishers for children

Raintree is an imprint of Capstone Global Library Limited, a company incorporated in England and Wales having its registered office at 264 Banbury Road, Oxford, OX2 7DY – Registered company number: 6695582

www.raintree.co.uk
myorders@raintree.co.uk

Designed by Aruna Rangarajan and Tracy McCabe
Original illustrations © Capstone Global Library Limited 2020
Originated by Capstone Global Library Ltd
Printed and bound in India.

978 1 4747 8962 2 (paperback)

British Library Cataloguing in Publication Data
A full catalogue record for this book is available from the British Library.

Acknowledgements
We would like to thank the following for permission to reproduce design elements:
Shutterstock.

Contents

Something fishy

Pedro told his dad, "I'm doing something fishy today."

"You are?" asked his dad.

"Yes!" Pedro smiled. "I'm going to the aquarium."

His dad laughed. "That *is* fishy!"

"I've saved some money," said Pedro. "I'm bringing back a souvenir."

"Great!" said his dad. "I can't wait to see it."

At the aquarium, Miss Winkle told the class, "Make sure you stay together."

"That's easy," said Pedro. "We can pretend we are minnows. They always stick together."

"It's cool in here," said

Katie. "And dark."

"Yes," added JoJo. "It's a

bit spooky."

"Here comes something crabby!" said Pedro.

"Is it my baby brother?" joked Barry.

"Very funny!" said Miss Winkle. "It's a hermit crab."

"I love the starfish," said Katie. "They look dreamy."

"But the jellyfish looks lonely," said JoJo. "Maybe he's looking for a peanut butter fish."

"I'd love to have a ride on

the seahorse," said Pedro. "But

I would need to be smaller."

"Yes," said Katie. "And

don't forget your snorkel!"

Roddy ran ahead. "YAY!" he yelled. "Here come the sharks! *Duck!*"

"Yikes!" said Pedro. "Those teeth look sharp. I don't want to ride on *him.*"

"You know," said Pedro, "all this water is making me thirsty."

He walked away to find a water fountain.

Chapter 2
Alone with the shark

When Pedro finished

drinking, he looked for his

class. They were gone.

Pedro was alone – with

the shark!

"See you later!" Pedro yelled. "I have to find my class."

"Here they are!" he smiled.

"I can see JoJo!"

No! It wasn't her.

"I bet my class is around this corner," said Pedro.

The room was dark and filled with whales.

"Yay!" yelled Pedro. "Here's my class."

No! It *wasn't!*

Pedro ran

this way and

that way, but

he kept coming

back to the shark.

Pedro looked at the shark, who was swimming in circles.

"Ha!" Pedro smiled. "That's why I can't find my class! I've been going in circles. Thanks for the clue."

Chapter 3
Be like a turtle

Pedro tried a new direction.

He passed a sea turtle. She moved slowly, looking calm and wise.

"I'll try that," said Pedro.

Pedro took a deep breath.

He walked slowly. "I'll turn
left this time, then right."

Success! Pedro found his
class.

"There you are!" said Miss Winkle. "We were going to start searching."

"I found you first," Pedro said proudly.

When he got home, Pedro said, "Dad, come and see my souvenirs."

His dad smiled, "Why did you choose a shark and a sea turtle?"

"It's a long story," said

Pedro.

"Good," said his dad.

"You can tell me while we

walk Peppy."

Pedro's story was so long, they walked around the park twice.

"Sometimes," said Pedro, "it's fun to go in circles."

And it was!

About the author

Fran Manushkin is the author of many popular picture books, including *Happy in Our Skin*; *Baby, Come Out!*; *Latkes and Applesauce: A Hanukkah Story*; *The Tushy Book*; *Big Girl Panties*; and *Big Boy Underpants*. Fran writes on her beloved Mac computer in New York, USA, without the help of her two naughty cats, Chaim and Goldy.

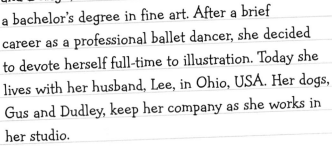

About the illustrator

Tammie Lyon began her love of drawing at a young age while sitting at the kitchen table with her dad. She continued her love of art and eventually attended the Columbus College of Art and Design, where she earned a bachelor's degree in fine art. After a brief career as a professional ballet dancer, she decided to devote herself full-time to illustration. Today she lives with her husband, Lee, in Ohio, USA. Her dogs, Gus and Dudley, keep her company as she works in her studio.

Glossary

aquarium place where collections of water animals and plants are kept and shown

minnows tiny freshwater fish

snorkel tube that you use to breathe through when you are swimming under water

souvenir object that you keep to remind you of a place, a person or an event

success good outcome

Let's talk

1. How could Pedro have avoided getting separated from his class?

2. How do you think Pedro felt when he realized he was lost?

3. Imagine you are Pedro and explain why you chose shark and sea turtle magnets for souvenirs.

Let's write

1. Write a list of all the sea animals in this story. Then draw a picture of your favourite one, and write a sentence about why it is your favourite.

2. Write a story about going on a field trip. It can be either a true story or something you've made up.

3. Write three facts about sharks. If you can't think of three, ask a grown-up to help you find some in a book or on the internet.

JOKE AROUND

⭐ What are a shark's favourite sweets?
jaw breakers

⭐ What do fish take to stay healthy?
vitamin sea

⭐ Who granted the fish's wish?
her fairy cod mother

⭐ Why did the shark cross the road?
to get to the other tide

⭐ What do sea monsters eat?
fish and ships

Where do fish keep their money?
in the river bank

Why won't the shrimp share its toys?
Because it's shellfish.

What day do fish hate?
fry-day

What's the most musical part of a fish?
the scales

What's the most famous fish in the ocean?
the starfish

THE FUN DOESN'T STOP HERE!

Discover more stories and characters at

www. raintree.co.uk